XTREME MYSTERIES

#6 Out of Line

Laban Hill

HYPERION PAPERBACKS FOR CHILDREN
NEW YORK

Prologue

Hoke Valley Network
Xtreme Sports Chatroom
Thursday 11:50 P.M.

 Xliner: *Hello.*
 Silence.
 Xliner: *Anybody here?*
 Silence again. No one else was in the chatroom. He thought he would leave a message anyway.
 Xliner: *Skaters rule! The new skate park must be built or all will suffer. Any feebs who resist will be taken care of. Nobody can stop the XLINER! He never sleeps. Ha, ha, ha, ha!*
 Xliner signed off. Hoke Valley Net's Xtreme Sports Chatroom was empty for the rest of the night.

"No way."

"Way." Thirteen-year-old Natalie Whittemore dropped into her friend Wall Evan's half pipe to prove she could hold an invert for more than three seconds. She had been practicing this trick for a month, and now she was ready to show it off.

She screamed down the wall on her in-line skates. Like a rocket she shot up the opposite side and planted her hand hard on the lip. Her legs sprung like a coil and hurled her skates skyward. A gnarly invert.

"One one thousand . . ." Wall counted.

Nat's arm shook and trembled like a twig in a hurricane as she held the invert. She wasn't very big. Her face had a frail look to it, but that hid the fact that she had an iron will and was in great shape. Like Wall, she spent much of her spare time doing extreme sports.

" . . . *two one thousand . . . three one thousand.*"

Boom! Nat's blades thumped on the plywood wall.

She dropped into a tuck to maintain her balance and whipped up the other wall. A quick turn around to pick up speed, she rolled up the opposite wall again and slid her skates along the lip in a perfect soul.

"Groovy!" Wall cheered.

"Groovy?" Kevin Schultz shouted from the edge of the driveway. He had on in-line skates while Jamil Smith who was with him was riding a skateboard. They had just arrived at Wall's house. Nat, Wall, Jamil, and Kevin were the X-crew, four kids who loved extreme sports and solving mysteries. "What kind of word is groovy? Is this the sixties or something?"

Wall grinned. "My dad said it the other day. I liked it." Wall strutted over to his friends and gave Kevin and Jamil high fives. "Groovy rules, bro."

"I'll have to grow a massive afro if I start saying groovy," Kevin joked. His black kinky hair was cropped close to his skull.

"S'up?" Jamil cut in.

Nat hopped out of the pipe and walked across the grass in her skates. "Showing Wall that in-liners are just as sick as skateboarders."

Wall held up his hands. "She won! I promise. I won't ever dis in-line skates again."

Nat smiled with satisfaction. "If you think that was good, just get Ewan over here. He'll show you what aggro liners can do." Ewan McKindrick was the most radical in-line skater in Hoke Valley, Colorado. He was a sophomore at the high school. Nat met him on the planning committee for the new skate park.

"Agh! Ewan again!" Jamil cried. "Ever since you got on that committee all you do is talk about Ewan. So he rocks on skates. That's really cool, but enough already."

Nat blushed. She hadn't realized how much she'd been talking about Ewan. Luckily, a barking dog drew everyone's attention away from Nat's red face.

"Woof! Woof!" a golden retriever trotted over, and rubbed his nose against Jamil's hand.

"Hey!" Jamil said. "I thought I told you to get lost."

"Who's that?" Wall asked his friend.

Jamil knelt down and scratched behind the dog's ears. The dog's hair was matted with leaves and sticks like it had been living out in the woods. "He was outside the senior center when I left. I gave him a few cookies that a lady had given me. Now, I can't seem to get rid of him."

The retriever licked Jamil's face.

"Yuck!"

"I hope there wasn't any chocolate in the cookies," Nat said. "Chocolate's deadly for dogs."

"No," Jamil assured her. "Plain oatmeal."

"Did you sell any T-shirts?" Nat asked. She had enlisted Jamil in her fund-raising efforts for the new skate park. The committee had decided to sell T-shirts. It was Nat's idea to hit the senior center. Initially, Jamil had been reluctant. He didn't think old folks would be interested in buying T-shirts for a skate park.

"I bow at your feet, O perfect one," Jamil replied.

"Every person at the center bought one." Jamil vigorously rubbed the dog's neck. "Isn't that right, fella?"

The dog panted, his tongue lolling out of the side of his mouth.

Nat tried not to gloat. Because of her efforts, the committee was approaching one thousand T-shirts sold.

"I can't tell where the dog ends and you begin, Jamil," Kevin cracked. "You've both got dreadlocks." Jamil's blond dreadlocks were the same color as the dog's matted hair.

"Don't start with the hair jokes, Kev," Jamil replied. "How many T-shirts have *you* sold?"

A sheepish grin spread across Kevin's face. "A big fat zero. I've been too wrapped up in my science project. Which reminds me . . . I came over here to show you this cool trick." He slipped off his backpack and rummaged around inside. He pulled out a glass, a bottle of water, a white piece of paper, and a piece of white cardboard with a half-inch slit down the center. His friends followed him over to the picnic table beside the pipe. The dog followed and lay down underneath it.

Kevin filled the glass with water and then placed the card upright against the glass so that the sun shone through the slit and water onto the white paper.

"A rainbow!" Wall exclaimed. "How'd you do that?"

"Refraction. The water bends the light's wavelengths so you can see all the colors in light," Kevin explained. "It's part of my project for Mr. Clary's class."

Nat groaned. "I haven't even started mine. It's not due for three weeks, right?"

Kevin nodded. "But I wanted to get started, so I can enter this in the state science fair." He dumped the water into the grass and put the stuff back in his backpack. "I got next!" In his skates he ran ducklike to the pipe.

Kevin skated back and forth in the pipe until he had gathered enough momentum to reach the lip. As always, Kevin's skates were the most radical ones on the market. They had a combined hard and soft shell with a power arch. His parents owned Alpine Sports, a local sporting goods store, and that meant he was usually geared up to the max.

He kicked his left heel against the lip at the top of one wall and sailed about three feet. His right leg quickly crossed over his left as he wrapped the tips of his fingers around the wheels of his right skate.

"Rockin' lu kang!" Nat cheered. "Uh-oh!" Nat put her hands over her face. Kevin was not going to land his trick.

Crash!

But the sound of metal hitting pavement drowned out the hard thud of Kevin's landing.

The metal garbage can beside the back door of the house rolled on the pavement. Rotting banana peels and other kitchen garbage tumbled out as the dog tore into plastic bags of garbage.

"Hey! Get out of there!" Mike Evans, Wall's dad, shouted angrily as he banged open the back door.

The retriever skittered away like he was about to be hit, his tail tucked tightly between his legs.

"Whose dog is this?" Mr. Evans demanded.

The golden retriever retreated to Jamil's side.

"Is that your dog, Jamil?"

"Uh . . . well . . . kind of . . . ," Jamil stuttered. "He followed me home and I can't get rid of him."

"Well, keep him out of my garbage," Mr. Evans said curtly. "Wall, I want you and your friends to clean this mess up."

"Sure, Dad," Wall said.

"Mr. Evans, do you know what time it is?" Nat asked.

Mr. Evans glanced at his watch. "Almost four."

"I've got to jet, guys," Nat said as she started skating toward the street.

"Hey! My dad said we all have to clean up!" Wall shouted after her.

Nat spun to a stop and put her hands up in the air. "Sorry, but I've got a meeting at the Zoning Board. They're going to decide whether we can have the park or not."

"Then, go!" Wall called after her. "Just remember to meet up at the football game. You promised you'd come this time."

Nat waved as she took off.

"Beat it!" Jamil waved his arms to scare the retriever away, but the dog just stood there. He barked and wagged his tail. In frustration, Jamil picked up a stick and threw it.

With a long, loping stride, the retriever took off after it. He picked up the stick in his mouth and returned it to Jamil.

"Looks like he thinks you want to play," Kevin observed.

"Dumb dog," Jamil muttered. He grabbed the trash can lid off the grass.

Wall turned the can upright. "Hey, you guys want to play Zorched?" Zorched was the hottest game on the Internet. Players create their own characters and choose special powers in order to traverse a strange futuristic world.

"Yeah!" Jamil said as he banged the lid on top of the garbage can and snapped the latch. "This ought to keep him out of it."

Kevin sat on the steps leading to the back door and unlaced his skates. "Let's rock it."

Inside Wall's bedroom they waited for the computer to log on the Hoke Valley Net, otherwise known as the HVNet, the local Internet server.

"I hope Nat's meeting goes well," Kevin said. "I could really go for a skate park with rad obstacles."

"Yeah, it would finally give us a real place to skate," Jamil replied.

"Thanks," Wall replied.

"Oops. You know what I mean," Jamil said. "Your halfpipe is heavy stuff. But having a real park would be so awesome."

"Yeah, I know," Wall said. "I want a park too. I can't stand riding on the flat playground. It's so boring!" He hit a couple of keys and clicked his mouse on a window. "Let's check out the Xtreme Chatroom first."

"Cool," Kevin said.

Wall clicked on his bookmark icon. He zoomed down the list and double clicked on Xtreme Sports Chatroom. The chatroom's window opened and Wall's on-line name got posted: WallIt. Three others were also logged into the chatroom.

"Hey, Ian and Mark are here," Jamil exclaimed.

Wall bristled. A few months earlier, he had beaten out Mark in a drawing contest that turned into a heavy mystery. Ever since, he and Mark hadn't spoken to each other. Ian was a radical bmxer who had his own pipe in a barn on his parents' property. "Who's Xliner?"

"Don't know," Jamil replied. Xliner was the third person in the chatroom.

"Me neither," Kevin said. "Ask him who he is."

Wall hit a few keys.

Xliner—stats?

A few seconds passed.

The most down in-line sk8er on planet Hoke Valley. Go hard, go big, dude!

"Get a load of this guy," Jamil cracked. "Ask him if he's amped about the skate park?"

Wall smiled as he typed.

Sk8 dude. You cranked for the new skate park to open?

He replied:

Wheels are burning, but word is football feebs are putting up a major fight. If they do, it's lights out for them!

Wall typed quickly:

Groovy!

"This is a total snore," Kevin complained. "Let's get Zorched!"

"Just a sec," Wall said as he typed more.

The skate park rules!

Wall clicked out and opened his bookmark menu again. "Do you really think they'll stop the park?" Wall said, slightly worried.

"No way," Jamil replied. "The money's been raised and even the mayor is behind it."

The fire-breathing dragon of Zorched appeared on the screen and blasted fire. The screen burst into flames and dissolved into the setup menu.

Nat stood with the refrigerator door open and stared. Her right arm was draped over the door. She had stopped off at home on her way to the zoning board meeting.

Before her were nearly empty shelves. There were just a few things—a jug of milk, an apple, leftover spaghetti, a bag of carrots, and a container of cottage cheese with an expiration date that had passed the previous week. Nat's parents weren't too plugged in to maintaining the perfect household. They spent much of their time in the bookstore they owned, just below their apartment. Her dad, Jake Whittemore, was an excellent cook, but he hadn't had a chance to shop for supplies in about a week. Her mom, Wendy Whittemore, was the kind of person who would stand over the sink and eat dry cereal out of the box so she didn't have to dirty a dish.

"Is that you, Nat?" Mr. Whittemore called up the stairs from the store.

"Yeah, Dad."

Mr. Whittemore came upstairs into the apartment. He wore thick glasses with a safety pin holding the earpiece to the frame. His dress shirt had a coffee stain on the front. He was usually too distracted with his thoughts to notice the state of his clothes. Nat wasn't quite so sloppy. In many ways, Nat wasn't like her parents at all. She liked being outside doing things. Her little sister, Ella, was more like them. She usually hung out in the back of the store reading after school.

When Mr. Whittemore saw Nat leaning into the fridge, he said, "Sorry about the food situation. I was just about to leave for the grocery store. You want anything special?"

"Food," Nat moaned dramatically. She grabbed a carrot and began peeling it over the sink.

"Okay, I get the hint," Mr. Whittemore replied. "I'll go right now." He grabbed his jacket and headed for the door. It had started getting cool in the late afternoon as autumn approached.

"I'll walk with you," Nat said as she ran to catch up to him. She slung her skates over her shoulder and zipped her hooded sweatshirt. "I've got a zoning board meeting on the skate park."

Mr. Whittemore beamed. He was proud of his daughter's activism.

As Nat mentioned the meeting, she was reminded that Ewan would be there. For a moment, she hesitated about getting advice from her dad. But then, as usual, she plunged ahead. "Dad?"

"Yeah?" Mr. Whittemore put his hands in his jacket pockets and jingled his keys.

"Um . . . if you like someone, how do you let them know?" Nat said in a near whisper.

"I guess you just try to be their friend," Mr. Whittemore replied. "You invite them to do stuff and you help them out when they need it."

That wasn't exactly the answer Nat was looking for, but she was too embarrassed to explain what she meant. They walked a couple of blocks in silence.

"You'll be home for supper?" Mr. Whittemore asked as they approached the corner.

Nat shook her head. "I promised the gang I'd meet them at the football game. Can I have a couple of bucks for hot dogs?"

Mr. Whittemore dug into his pocket. He gave her five dollars. "This is your allowance, remember, so don't ask for more."

Nat stuffed the five in her pocket. Disappointed, she hoped she could get away with the money not counting as her weekly allowance.

Nat and her father parted company.

Bang! Bang! The zoning board's chairperson's gavel hit the tabletop to call everyone to attention. "This hearing on the proposed skateboard park to be built next to the Hoke Valley High School football field is now in session," announced Chairperson Adam Jacobson, who was dressed in a navy pin-striped business suit. He was a local real estate broker and contractor and, like everyone else, volunteered his time on the board.

On the dais an older woman with thick glasses leaned into the mike in front. "And let's make this brief. We've got the Homecoming football game tonight." The nameplate in front of her read Betty Gill.

A murmured agreement swept across the room.

Nat turned around and saw that the room was packed, at least fifty people. "I hope they're not all football fans," muttered Nat to Ewan McKindrick who was sitting right next to her. They both were seated in the first row behind the podium where the people who had signed up to speak would testify. Nat was thrilled to be next to him, but at the same time she was terrified of saying or doing something that would make Ewan think she was a total feeb.

"They better not be, or we're in deep trouble," Ewan replied as he sunk into his chair.

"Why?"

"Football has got to be the dumbest sport. I played last year as a wide receiver. This year, though, when the coach found out I was skating all the time, he had a cow," Ewan explained. "He told me if I continued skating during the season, he'd throw me off the team." Ewan shrugged. "So I got thrown off the team." Ewan's jaw tightened as he said this.

"That's bent," Nat replied. "I just can't figure out why anybody would want to do a sport that's so limiting."

"It was like being in prison," Ewan added. He glanced around the room. "See that guy over there?"

Nat followed his gaze. At the back of the room stood a massive man dressed in a red sports coat and a black vinyl cap. "Yeah?"

"That's Coach Hamilton. People in town think he's a god," Ewan said sullenly. "If he's against the park, then we don't have a chance. No one would ever think of going against him. He's been the coach for thirty years."

"But we got the mayor on our committee," Nat responded, slightly worried.

"Doesn't matter. If Coach Ham doesn't want it, then it won't happen," Ewan said firmly.

"You're being paranoid." Nat glanced back at the coach again. She noticed a kid with red hair standing beside him. The kid was wearing a huge flower corsage. Weird, she thought.

Chairperson Jacobson continued. "The issues on the table tonight are first whether to build the skate park on the open acre of land behind the football field and second when to begin construction if the park is approved. Let's have people from the skate park committee speak, and then those who oppose the park. Margaret, would you start please?"

Mayor Margaret Masters approached the podium, "Thank you, Adam." She pulled a set of design plans from her briefcase and handed copies to the board members. "This is the proposed design for the park. As you can see, it fits perfectly in the space behind the football field. Traffic for the park wouldn't interfere at all with the games."

"Will the park have lights for night skating?" Mr. Jacobson asked.

"No," answered Mayor Masters. "Let me draw your attention to the efficient use of the site." She pointed out several features in the design that integrated the park into the landscape.

"Won't this park just encourage a bad element in the community?" asked Francis Teagarten, another committee member.

Don't forget the visitors' argument, Nat said to herself.

"Just the opposite," the mayor replied. "It will give

kids a place to skate. Skaters won't have to practice in front of stores." Teagarten nodded. He owned Muddy Waters, a coffee shop in the open-air Main Street Market that ran down Main Street. Many of the store owners in the mall had complained about skateboarders and in-liners blocking the stores from paying customers.

Mayor Masters wrapped up her presentation with a request that they begin construction immediately. "It is important to finish before the November construction cut-off date." Since they depended so much on winter vacationers, all road and building construction was restricted from November to April in Hoke Valley.

Mayor Masters returned to her seat.

"Wait!" Nat leaped up from her seat. "The park could also be a draw in the summer for vacationers. We could have competitions in conjunction with the Bear Claw Mountain Bike Races. The nearest skate park is in Denver. We would be the only resort town to have one."

The board members stared at Nat like she was a bug.

Chairperson Jacobson glanced down at his list of speakers. "And you are?"

"Natalie Whittemore, sir," Nat said nervously.

Chairperson Jacobson paused. "Your name is not listed to speak this evening. Please sit down."

Nat slid back into her chair. "But I'm on the skate park committee with the mayor and she forgot one of the points we had decided to present."

The mayor put her hand gently on Nat's shoulder and whispered into her ear. "Cyrus is set to give that testimony." Cyrus McGowan owned Rumble Boards, the local snowboarding and skateboarding shop.

Nat blushed. Now she had made a fool of herself in front of Ewan. She tried to disappear into her seat.

"It doesn't matter, anyway," Ewan muttered.

Nat smiled. She appreciated Ewan ignoring her gaff.

"The skate park isn't going to be built," Ewan continued. "Adam Jacobson was the star quarterback on Coach Ham's only team to make it to the state finals. There's no way he'd let the park be built if the coach is against it."

Nat glanced at Ewan with surprise. She couldn't believe how negative he was. At committee meetings in the past, he had always been upbeat about the park.

"Cyrus, are you ready?" Chairperson Jacobson asked.

Cyrus came to the podium and began his presentation. When he finished, he returned to his seat.

"It's getting late," Ms. Gill said as she looked at her watch. The clock on the wall said 5:00 P.M. The football game began at 7:00 P.M. "We better get Coach Ham up first so he can get to the game."

"Good point," Chairperson Jacobson replied. "Coach Ham, would you like to speak now?"

"Thank you, Adam," the coach said as he made his way down the aisle. "I just have one point to make. Football has a long history in this town. It's a sport that teaches kids discipline and teamwork. This skate park is a distraction for the kids. The money would be better served invested in a football program for the junior high."

A number of people in the audience seconded this.

After the coach left, people in opposition to the park spoke. By 6:30 P.M. the testimony was finished.

"That seems to be it," Mr. Jacobson said.

"Uh, Mr. Chairman," Ms. Gill interrupted.

"Yes, Betty?"

"I move that we have a vote right now on the park," she said.

"I second that," Mr. Teagarten added.

"Okay, all those in favor of voting on the park right now, raise your hands," Mr. Jacobson said. He glanced up and down the table at the other board members. Everyone on the board but Jacobson voted yes. "The board has voted to decide the matter now, so we'll vote." He paused. "Everyone in favor of the skate park, raise your hands."

Again, everyone on the committee but Mr. Jacobson voted yes.

"All right!" Nat shouted as she leaped from her seat and clapped furiously.

Mr. Jacobson looked stunned. "I guess it's settled," he said. "Except for the date of the groundbreaking. I move that we table that discussion until next week."

"Second," one board member said quickly.

The board voted unanimously to table the groundbreaking date until the next meeting.

"This meeting is adjourned." Mr. Jacobson banged his gavel. "We've got a football game to watch!"

"Don't get excited," Ewan told Nat. "The board could still vote to delay the groundbreaking for a hundred years. It's not over until the bulldozers start digging."

"Don't be so negative," Nat said. "We just have to convince the committee to start construction right away!"

"Just," Ewan replied.

Nat followed him out of the hearing room. She contemplated inviting Ewan to the game with her and the guys.

As they stepped outside, the red-haired kid with the corsage came up. "Hey, Ewan, smell my flower." He leaned into Ewan and water squirted from the corsage into Ewan's face.

"Give it a rest, Roman," Ewan said impatiently. "Your pranks aren't that funny to me."

Roman broke up laughing, like he had just told the funniest joke in the world.

Ewan glanced up the street. "I've got to jet."

"Wait," Nat cried. "I'm going to the game with some friends. You want to come?"

"I've got something to do," Ewan said.

Nat stood there, disappointed that Ewan had taken off so fast. She really liked hanging with him. Not only was he a rad skater, but she felt good when she was around him. She had never felt like this with a boy before.

"You want to smell?" Roman squirted Nat with water.

Nat wiped the water off her face. "Very funny."

"Thanks," he replied. "I've got to suit up for the game." He took off down the street.

"Like I care," Nat said to his back.

"Don't lose your ticket. There'll be a drawing at halftime for a year's supply of motor oil, sponsored by the Auto Advantage," the ticket seller told Nat after she paid her twenty-five cents.

"Thanks, Mrs. Grenon. I sure need a year's supply of motor oil," Nat said as she crossed her eyes.

Mrs. Grenon laughed.

Nat headed for the stands. She had agreed to meet Kevin, Wall, and Jamil in the top row. As she climbed, she could see her friends had already arrived. "Hey!"

Jamil waved. "Hurry up!"

Nat took the stairs two at a time, dodging people as she went. The Hoke Valley side of the stadium was packed while the visitors' side was only half full.

The stadium lights made the field as bright as day. The humming sound they made caught Kevin's attention. "Those are arc lights. Their light comes from infrared rays that are at the bottom of the light spectrum and normally unseen."

"Good to know, Kev," Jamil deadpanned.

"Yeah, Kev, I'm sure I can use that information," added Nat.

Kevin shrugged. "I can't help it. Infrared and ultraviolet light are what my science project is about. I'm going to do some cool stuff with black lights and arc lights."

"Black lights!" Wall said. "Groovy. My dad's got these posters from when he was a kid. When he shines a black light onto them they look really cool. They kind of jump off the wall. Very groovy."

"Ladies and gentleman, your Hoke Valley Miners," the speaker above them barked.

The crowd gave the team a standing ovation as they ran onto the field.

"This is crazy!" Nat shouted to her friends. "I didn't know football was so big." She dropped her in-line skates on the bleachers next to her friends' skates and skateboards.

"Major," Kevin answered. "My parents sell the jerseys and equipment to the team. They make so much money from tickets and concessions that they can afford to buy new uniforms every year."

"A money machine," Wall said.

"No kidding," Kevin replied. "Next week they're going to replace the scoreboard."

"Your parents sell them that too?" Nat asked.

"Naw, that comes from a company that specializes in

those types of things," Kevin said. "But I bet my dad wishes he did. Jacobson Construction is putting it up, though."

"Jacobson Construction? Is that the same Jacobson who's on the Zoning Board?" Nat asked.

Kevin nodded.

"Isn't that a conflict of interest?" Nat asked.

"I guess," Kevin replied.

"This is not good," Nat said, shaking her head. "Ewan might be right."

"Right about what?" Wall asked Nat.

Nat explained to her friends what Ewan had said after the zoning board meeting. "If Jacobson is so tight with the coach and he's the zoning board chairperson, he'll probably find some way to block the skate park." Nat slumped on the bleacher seat and ran her hands through her long blond hair.

Jamil leaned over the back rail of the stadium and whistled. "Hey, Buddy!"

"Buddy? Who's Buddy?" Nat asked.

"That's what he named the dog," Wall explained.

Jamil turned. "Since I can't get rid of him, I figured I better name him. He's right down there."

Nat looked over the rail and saw Buddy standing by the bleachers. "When's the game start? I want to find out why so many people like to watch football. I just don't get it."

"I think football's pretty cool," Wall said. "I mean you get to slam into people."

Nat looked at him funny. Sometimes she couldn't figure Wall out. "Oh, *that* sounds like a lot of fun . . . not."

"No really, how often do you get to just lay into someone and not get in trouble?" Wall tried to explain.

"Well, if my sister played, then maybe I'd like slamming into her." Nat laughed.

"I'm with Nat," Jamil put in. "I don't get football either."

"Just watch the game, you'll see. It's fun," said Kevin. "I really like playing catch with my dad."

"Me, too," added Wall. "The game's about to start."

The two teams were lined up on the field for the kickoff.

"Who're we playing?" Nat asked.

"The Miners are kicking off to the Padden Panthers," Kevin said.

"That's Roman Jacobson." Wall pointed at the kicker for the Miners.

"Is his dad the same Jacobson we've just been talking about?" Nat asked.

"One and the same," Kevin replied. "And Roman thinks he's the funniest guy on the planet. The only problem is . . . nobody else agrees with him."

Nat knew exactly what Kevin meant.

Roman ran up to the tee and kicked the football high into the air. A Panther fielded the ball and got behind the wedge his teammates formed.

The two teams collided into each other, but somehow a Panther broke free. He dashed straight for the end zone. Roman went after him, but the runner juked him good. Touchdown Panthers.

"Serves him right," Nat muttered.

"But the Miners are now losing," Wall replied. "I don't care what a jerk Roman is. I don't want the Miners to lose, especially on homecoming night." But Wall's wish didn't seem to be coming true. The first half ended: Panthers 14, Miners 0.

"They'll catch them in the second half," Kevin said hopefully.

Hoke Valley High's marching band came onto the field, followed by a dozen miniature cars driven by grown men wearing fezzes with tassels hanging from the top.

"Who are those guys?" Wall asked.

"The Shriners." Kevin laughed. "They drive those funny cars around and try to raise money for their children's hospitals around the country. They show up at every parade in town."

"They should lose the hats," Wall replied.

"I don't want to sit up here and watch those guys drive around in cars," Jamil said.

Nat glanced over at the steps of the high school. "Hey! Some kids are skating over there. Let's go!" Nat and her friends snagged their skates and skateboards. They took the stadium stairs two at a time.

At that moment, a convertible was pulling onto the field with the homecoming queen and king. They were about to be crowned.

Kevin glanced up at the clock over the scoreboard. "We've got fifteen minutes before the game starts again."

Nat and Kevin tied on their skates in the parking lot.

"Meet you over there," Wall called as he hopped on his deck. Jamil was right behind him. They ollied onto the sidewalk and kicked with their back foot a couple of times to pick up speed. Then Wall came off the curb, kickflipped his deck, and stuck the landing. Jamil followed, but crashed.

Nat and Kevin whipped by Jamil as he stood.

Suddenly, Nat pulled up by dragging her skate. "Hey! Look at that!" Nat shouted.

At the top of the stairs to the school, a skater in a hooded sweatshirt approached the railing slowly. As he came up beside the rail, he jumped into the air and twisted his shoulders to the right. His feet followed as he rose steadily into the air. When he faced up rail, his skates rose to the rail's height. The sole of his right skate locked against the rail. He shifted his weight over the right side of the rail and grabbed his left skate for balance and style. Then he slid backward down the rail on his right skate. His grinding leg locked in its bent position, he rode the entire length of the rail. At the bottom he hopped off and rolled backward for a few feet as he caught his balance. He skated off in the direction away from Nat and her friends.

"Honker trick!" Wall exclaimed. "He took that on one skate. I'm beginning to like this in-line stuff."

"Total stylin'," Kevin added. "Wasn't that a true spin to alley oop makio?"

"You got that right—as smooth as butter," Nat replied. "That rail must be twenty feet long."

Jamil came up beside Nat. "Wasn't that Ewan?"

"Really?" Nat said with surprise. "I couldn't see who it was underneath the hooded sweatshirt. I got to check it out." She skated away from the steps in the direction the rad in-liner went. "Rock you later, guys."

"I've got to ride that rail," Wall said. "I bet I can take it with a fifty-fifty."

"In your dreams!" Jamil cracked.

Wall took off up the steps with a skateboard in his hand. At the top he raised his board over his head and shouted. "I rule!"

His friends laughed.

"Fat chance!" someone yelled from behind Wall.

Wall spun around and saw a kid about his age skate by him. The kid wore a hooded sweatshirt just like the first skater. As he came up on the railing, he sprung like a coil and popped a suislide. But it only lasted half a second. Just as he straightened his right leg and reached for a grab, his body followed his shoulder and he spilled like yesterday's milk onto the steps.

"Splat!" Wall cracked.

Down below, Jamil turned to Kevin. "Isn't that Rocket Sinclair?"

"Yeah. He's probably here for the game. He lives in Padden," Kevin answered.

"Hey, Rocket!" Jamil waved. "You need better thrusters to take a suislide."

"Ha! Ha!" Rocket replied. He stood and walked down the steps. At the bottom he looked up at Wall. "Show us what you got, dude!"

Wall smiled. He backed away about a hundred feet to get some speed. As he came to the rail he ollied up into a perfect fifty-fifty grind. His front and back trucks were locked on the metal rail like they were superglued. As he rode the rail, sparks flew out from behind in the dim light.

"We'll have to come back and videotape him doing this. It's too cool not to preserve for eternity," Jamil said.

Nat skated behind the visitors' bleachers. She thought she spotted Ewan on the other side of the refreshment stand, but she couldn't reach him through the crowd before he disappeared again. She skated back toward the parking lot, thinking he might be leaving. She picked up speed and snaked through people returning to the stands. As she came around a corner behind the stadium, she thought she heard a dog barking behind her. She turned to see if it was Buddy.

Crunch!

Nat ran smack into Roman Jacobson dressed in his football pads. She bounced off him like a pinball.

"Hey, watch where you're going," Roman cried. Then he passed her without even giving her a hand.

Nat steamed for a minute as she sat on the pavement. Then she heard the dog barking again. She stood up and continued into the parking lot. Ewan was skating back toward the school with Jamil's dog nipping at his heels.

Nat still wanted to catch up to Ewan, but now she felt kind of silly for following him. She couldn't imagine what she would say to him. She turned and went back to the stands. The crowning ceremony of the homecoming king and queen was just wrapping up. The game would start in a couple of minutes.

Nat sat on the steps of the bleachers to take off her skates. People walked around her, heading back to their seats. She unlaced the first skate and slid it off. She rubbed her foot and wiggled her toes. No matter how much she skated, her feet still felt stiff and tired when she took her skates off.

Suddenly, the entire stadium was dark. Every light went out.

In shock, everyone stopped talking. It was like the loss of power not only put out the lights, but shut off the voices of everyone in the stadium as well.

The silence didn't last long, however. Within seconds a murmur rose from the crowd as everyone tried to find out what had happened.

Someone got on the loudspeaker to calm people down. "The lights will be back on momentarily. Just stay where you are."

Nat swallowed hard and tried to think of what to do. She did not want to stay seated on the bench until the lights went back on. She figured her first course of action should be to hook up with her friends. Although the loss of power was probably an accident, it could be the beginning of a new mystery. If it was, she wanted the X-crew to be in the thick of it.

Nat stood and carefully made her way off the bleachers. It was slow going because she couldn't see her or other people's toes very well. She finally came to the end and hopped down. She last saw Jamil, Wall, and Kevin by the steps leading to the entrance to the high school. She decided to look there.

To Nat's surprise, the lights in the parking lot were still on. It was just the stadium lights that had gone out. Many of the spectators had gathered among their cars. Nat edged along the outside of the crowd toward the

Feinberg's flying!

In-line skater Aaron Feinberg

After watching his friend skate for the first time, Aaron Feinberg decided to give Rollerblading a try. He began skating in Miami, FL, in 1994, and was soon hooked on the sport. Aaron's first competition was the National In-Line Skating Series (N.I.S.S.) in Miami. In early 1997, at the X Trials competition in Rhode Island, Aaron placed third and qualified as a professional skater. Soon after, he placed second at the Ultimate In-Line Challenge in Orlando, FL. But Aaron's latest and greatest victory was at the 1997 X Games in San Diego, CA—on his birthday, Aaron received the gold medal!

Aaron now lives in Portland, OR, but he spends much of his time traveling around the world participating in various in-line skating competitions.

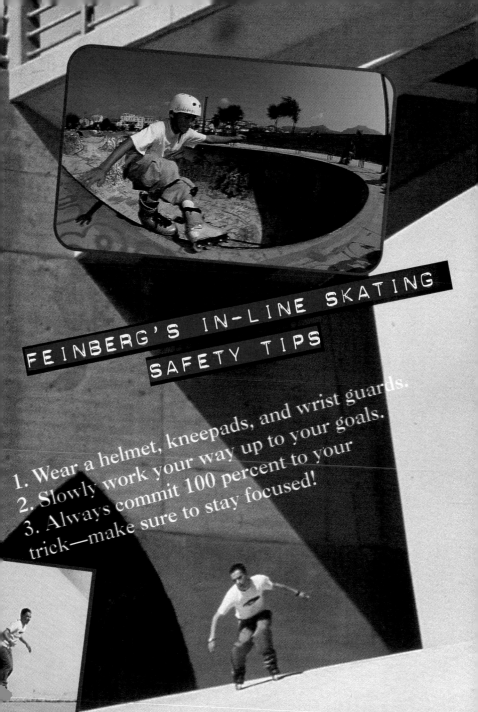

FEINBERG'S IN-LINE SKATING SAFETY TIPS

1. Wear a helmet, kneepads, and wrist guards.
2. Slowly work your way up to your goals.
3. Always commit 100 percent to your trick—make sure to stay focused!

Aaron at age 5

Age: 16

Most memorable competition: The X Games, because it was on my birthday and I won!

Favorite athlete: Arlo Eisenberg because he's the living legend of Rollerblading.

Favorite in-line skate: Salomon

What I like best about my sport: The atmosphere is more fun than competitive—we're all good friends.

Favorite thing to do on a Saturday: Go Rollerblading out in the streets or at a skate-park with my friends.

Favorite pig-out food: Sushi or clams

Favorite movie: *Space Balls*

steps. She couldn't spot her friends. She hoped they were still over there and bounced on the balls of her feet to see over people's heads.

Suddenly, a hand clamped on to her shoulder and she leapt higher than she had ever jumped before. Her heart nearly stopped as well.

Nat spun around. Standing right behind her were her friends—Jamil, Wall, and Kevin.

"That scare you?" Jamil smiled. He knew he caught her by surprise and was enjoying every second of it.

Nat coughed. "I was looking for you guys. Do any of you know what happened?"

"Yeah, the lights went out," Wall replied.

"Good answer, Sherlock. Did you figure that out by yourself?" Nat cracked.

"With the help of my esteemed colleagues," said Wall.

Just then, the high school assistant principal, Mr. Brooks, spoke over a bullhorn. "Attention! The game has been canceled. The lights cannot be repaired tonight. I'm sorry, but you'll have to go home."

Scattered boos and groans of disappointment erupted through the crowd. People started getting into their cars and driving away.

For a few minutes, the crew watched the spectators leave.

"What next?" Kevin asked.

"Hold on a second!" Jamil suddenly shouted. "Kevin! Wall! Don't you remember what we read in the chatroom this afternoon?"

"Yeah, some kid raging about aggro in-liners," Wall said, not understanding where Jamil was going at all.

"Explain, please," Nat said impatiently.

"No, the guy . . . what was his name?" Jamil snapped his fingers trying to remember.

"Xliner," Kevin answered.

"Right. This Xliner dude made a threat. He said that if the skate park is blocked, he was going to put out the lights of the stadium," explained Jamil. "It makes perfect sense. Maybe he sabotaged the game."

"Maybe," Kevin said.

"Don't you remember what a head case this guy was?" Jamil persisted.

"Okay," Nat replied. "Let's talk to Mr. Brooks and see if we can get any corroboration." They headed toward Mr. Brooks.

Mr. Brooks was standing with Coach Ham.

"Mr. Brooks!" Kevin called.

Mr. Brooks looked over at the gang. "Yes, Kevin?" Kevin knew Mr. Brooks because he was a customer of his parents. Mr. Brooks walked over to them.

"What happened?" Kevin asked.

"Well, I'm not sure," said Mr. Brooks, "but our custodian said the cable to the fuse box has been cut."

"So it wasn't an accident?" Nat asked.

Mr. Brooks adjusted the knot of the tie before he answered. "Apparently not."

"I knew it! I just knew it," Jamil said triumphantly.

"What did you know?" Mr. Brooks asked.

Jamil stuttered. "Just that someone did it on purpose."

Mr. Brooks looked at Jamil suspiciously. "Well, if any of you know anything about this incident, you better report it or you could be in big trouble."

Nat, Jamil, Wall, and Kevin looked at each other. Should they tell Mr. Brooks about the Xliner threat in the chatroom this afternoon?

Not a chance! This was now the X-crew's mystery and they weren't ready to hand it over to someone else until they could hand it over on a silver platter. And that meant all wrapped up with a bow on top.

"Uh . . . we've got to run, Mr. Brooks," Nat said, backing away. She pulled at her friends' shirts. "Let's check out the Xtreme Sports Chatroom over at my apartment," she continued after they were out of Mr. Brooks's earshot.

"Woof! Woof!"

Jamil turned. Buddy had found them. "Come on, boy! We've got a mystery to solve."

"Woof!" Buddy ran in circles chasing his tail.

"I sure hope we don't end up chasing our own tails," Kevin cracked.

In no time, the crew was sitting around the computer in the back office of the Bookworm, the store that Nat's parents ran. She was methodically hitting keys and clicking on icons to boot up onto the HVNet.

"You've got mail!" the computer announced after Nat logged on. She moved the cursor to the mail icon.

"Skip the mail. Let's hit the chatroom," Kevin said impatiently.

Nat clicked on the people icon and then opened a series of windows until she was in. No one else was there.

"What do we do now?" Jamil asked.

"Wait," Wall said. And that's what they did.

Jamil drummed his fingers on the desk. "Let's check out his profile."

Nat moved through a series of windows until she got to Xliner's profile on the HVNet.

"It's blank!" Kevin said surprised. "I thought everyone had to have a profile."

"Me, too," Nat seconded.

"This is very strange," Wall said. "Let me try something." Nat got up and Wall took her seat in front of the computer. He quickly typed in a few codes and suddenly the subscriber list with names and addresses appeared on the screen.

"Whoa! How'd you do that?" Kevin asked.

Wall smiled. "I figured out the server's password. Actually, I kind of stumbled onto it. For some reason the security on this net is pretty lax."

"Well? Who is Xliner?" Nat asked impatiently. She leaned over Wall's shoulder to get a better look at the screen.

Wall scrolled quickly to the end of the subscriber list since it was in alphabetical order by screen name.

WallIt
Win8

34

Wonk264
Xerxes1
Zuzuzu

"Huh? Where's Xliner?" Nat asked.

"This doesn't make sense. If he uses the HVNet, he's got to be on this list," Wall said irritably. He keyed another password. "Nobody is supposed to get in here without one."

"But you did," Kevin reminded Wall.

"Technically, yes. But we logged onto the server under Nat's screen name. This guy's screen name isn't even listed. That means he's like a ghost. Officially, he doesn't exist," Wall explained.

"Maybe we should go back to the chatroom," Jamil suggested. "That seems to be our only lead."

Wall returned to the chatroom.

Two people were now in the chatroom. Neither was Xliner.

"Xliner's not here," Jamil said. "Do you think we should tell the police about him?"

The crew was silent for a couple of minutes.

"Let's see what we can come up with first," Kevin suggested. "I'd hate to go to the police without solid evidence. I mean, we don't even have evidence that Xliner ever appeared on HVNet. Wall showed there's no record of him."

"Yeah, the police might think we're just pulling a stunt," Wall added.

"More important," Nat argued, "is that I don't think we should give Coach Ham or Mr. Jacobson any more reasons why the park should be canceled. If they connect the lights in the stadium going out with the proposed skate park, that will play into their opinion that skaters are troublemakers. Ewan told me earlier that Coach Ham can't stand skaters. That's why he threw him off the football team."

"Well, who do you think Xliner is?" Jamil asked.

"Somebody who has a grudge against the football stadium or someone who thinks football is getting in the way of the skate park," Kevin concluded. "Either way, Nat is right. Coach Ham would definitely use this to show how wild skaters are."

"Then we'll keep quiet about what we know," Nat suggested.

"And we'll try to track this person down before he . . . ," Jamil began.

"Or she . . . ," Nat added.

"Yeah, or she, can do any more damage," Jamil said.

Eight A.M. Way early for Nat on a Saturday morning. But Nat hadn't slept well. The idea of an in-line skater linked to the lights going out at the game made her uneasy. So she had flopped around her bed like a beached fish, unable to find a comfortable spot.

She stared at the digital clock on her beside table for about fifteen minutes before deciding to get up. Her younger sister, Ella, lay snoring in a bed on the other side of the room.

Nat quietly swung her legs out of bed. She didn't want to wake up Ella for anything. She needed some peace and quiet. And if Ella woke up, there'd be no chance for that. Ella was a motormouth. Nat used to think she'd wear down or get hoarse or something, but that never happened. Ella just chattered away about any-thing—and everything.

Nat slipped her feet into her slippers and grabbed her

robe. She got out of her bedroom without making a noise and went down the hall to the kitchen.

"Morning, Scout," Mr. Whittemore greeted Nat. "You're up early." Mr. and Mrs. Whittemore were sitting in their robes at the breakfast table reading the paper. They didn't have to open the bookstore for another hour and a half.

Nat groaned and half waved. She wasn't up for conversation yet. She grabbed a bowl, a box of cereal, milk, and a spoon. She thought a bowl of cereal might give her some energy. She poured herself a glass of juice.

Her dad sat across from her with the paper held up to his face. Nat's eyes drifted to the back page of the section of paper her dad was reading. It was the editorial page, something she was less than a little interested in. Until she saw the lead editorial.

She reached across the table, and knocked over her juice. Ignoring it, she pulled the paper from her dad's hands.

"Natalie!" both her parents barked at her.

"Get a towel and wipe up your mess," Mrs. Whittemore admonished.

"Just a second," Nat replied. She quickly scanned the page.

Skate Delinquents Too Much for Hoke Valley
by Coach Thaddeus Hamilton

Last night, some juvenile delinquent sabotaged Hoke

Valley High School's homecoming game by cutting the power line to the fuse box. This caused all the lights in the stadium to go out. Last night's incident is just the kind of crime that I've feared ever since the skate park has been proposed. Kids who skateboard and in-line skate participate in unsupervised activities that can lead to delinquency. Kids needs adult guidance to teach them commitment to community and give them a moral yard-stick. . . .

"Ugh!" Nat groaned. The newspaper slipped from her fingers and fell into the puddle of juice.

"That's not what I meant," Mrs. Whittemore said as she watched the paper soak up the juice.

"Uh, sorry, Mom. I didn't mean to, but . . ." Nat pointed to the editorial. Her parents turned the paper around and began reading.

"Now I understand," Mrs. Whittemore said. "This is not good, is it?"

"That's a total understatement, Mom. It's disas-trous," Nat replied. "If Coach Ham gets his way, this could mean the end of the park. And if that happens, I'll die!"

"Don't be so dramatic," Mr. Whittemore said.

"I'm not!" complained Nat. "You just don't under-stand how hard we've worked." Nat left the kitchen hurt by her parents insensitivity. She started for her room, but then she remembered Ella was still in there. Instead, she detoured into the bathroom and sat on the toilet seat.

She brought her knees up to her chin and wrapped her arms around her legs.

She wished she could talk to Ewan about this. With the way he felt about Coach Ham, she knew he would understand her sense of panic. She considered looking up his phone number from the list of committee members, but on second thought she was too shy. What if he blew her off again? She didn't think she could take that.

As she sat in the bathroom running all this through her mind, it occurred to her that Coach Ham would have had to do some pretty fast writing to have that editorial ready for last night's paper.

How did he do that? Nat wondered to herself. It was already late when the game was canceled. He must have had other things to take care of first.

The more she thought about it, the more it seemed unlikely that Coach Ham could have written that editorial and gotten it in by the newspaper's deadline.

"He must have written it before the game!" Nat said out loud. She smacked her fist in the palm of her hand. "And if that's true, then he knew the power was going to be cut!"

Bang! Bang! Bang!

"Hey! Who's in there with you?" Ella shouted as she hammered against the bathroom door. "Open up."

Nat turned on the shower to drown out her sister's voice.

Nat dressed quickly to go outside and skate. She thought she might run into Ewan since he was always out skating. She also felt very antsy after reading that article in the newspaper and she didn't know what to do with her energy. Besides, even if she didn't run into Ewan, she definitely needed to get some practice in. She had a set of new grind plates that she wanted to check out.

Outside, there was a chill in the air. A breeze rummaged through the trees that lined the street. The leaves hadn't turned yet, but it wouldn't be long. Because Hoke Valley was up in the mountains, autumn always came early here.

Nat zipped up her fleece jacket and skated toward the junior high. This was everyone's favorite place to skate. Its flat expanse of blacktop and a couple of wheelchair access ramps with rails made it the best place to practice grinds and other tricks.

After a couple of blocks she turned the corner around the hardware store and saw the eight-foot-high chain-link fence that surrounded the blacktop. A few cars drove down the street.

The playground was empty. "Morning cartoons," Nat muttered. She never had the patience to sit in front of the TV, but most kids she knew could watch anything that wasn't news.

Nat shrugged and skated toward the wheelchair ramp. She thought she'd work on a suislide grind. It was the biggest and baddest trick that all the kids were doing on the aggro skate videos. She saw Kevin do it the day before and she couldn't help but feel a twinge of jealousy.

What made the suislide so sick was that a skater had to grind on the outside plate of the right foot while extending the left skate forward and making a grab. It sounded easy, but to find the right balance and timing was going to take a lot of work.

There was about ten feet to get up some speed at the top of the ramp. That was just enough. Nat didn't want to be going too slow. Otherwise, she'd stall when her skate made contact.

"Here goes nothing," Nat said to the empty playground.

She kicked her right skate. Then her left. Quickly she picked up speed. Before she knew it the curb running along the inside of the ramp was on her.

She held her breath. Jumped with her body facing forward.

Clack! Pointing her right skate inward, the outside edge of the grind plate locked onto the curb. With her weight a bit behind her and slightly to the side of the curb, she extended her left foot and grabbed.

"Oooo!" Nat grunted. Her face pitched forward. About to kiss the pavement, she quickly rolled her left shoulder forward and slid along her shoulder blade. Then she rolled out of the tuck and came to a stop. She crouched and checked out the damage.

Her T-shirt had a tear on its shoulder, but otherwise she was fine. No damage except a strawberry on her shoulder blade.

She repeated the trick several more times, but couldn't stick it. After about half an hour, she decided to call it quits.

"Too distracted," she said to herself, which was half true. She wanted to do something in response to Coach Ham's editorial before things got too out of hand. The other half was that she had to just practice. And she didn't always have the patience to fall over and over again until she got it right.

Nat skated back up the ramp. She figured she'd at least end on a success. She pulled off a super good torque soul. Both her skates locked on the outside and slid like the curb was buttered all the way down. Then she headed straight for home.

Nat ignored the stairs leading from the street up to her family's apartment and banged through the front door of the bookstore.

"Hey! No skates, Scout!" Mr. Whittemore called to Nat.

Nat waved and walked like a duck to the back office. She knew she was going to catch it for walking through the store in skates, but she just couldn't stop to take them off. She had to call Mayor Masters.

She dialed. The phone rang a couple of times before it was answered.

"Hello?" said a woman's voice on the other end of the line.

"Mayor?" Nat asked.

"Yes. Is this Nat?" Mayor Masters asked.

"Did you see the coach's editorial this morning?" Nat replied.

"I've been answering calls about it all morning," explained the mayor.

"What are we going to do?" Nat asked.

"I'm already composing a response to appear in tomorrow's paper. But if he has evidence to connect the cutting of the power line at the stadium to skaters, then the skate park will be in real trouble."

"Anything I can do?"

"No. I'm calling a special meeting for Monday evening of the skate park committee to plan a response," said the mayor. "Try not to worry."

Nat couldn't help but worry because the mayor didn't know what she knew. The coach could be right. It could have been a skater. At least, that's if her friends were right about what they had read in the chatroom the day before.

Nat fired up the computer and logged into the chatroom. Besides her, no one was there. Lost in thoughts about the skate park, she sat and stared at the ceiling for a few minutes. When her eyes came back to the screen, she realized she wasn't alone anymore.

Xliner had arrived.

NatSk8: *What up aggro dude?*
Xliner: *Did you rock the lights at the stadium last night?*

Nat tried to decide whether to chew him out about that stunt or lead him into thinking that she was of like mind. Maybe then she could get him to reveal who he really was.

NatSk8: *LOL. Totally sick. Did you do that?*
Xliner: *Roses are red,*
violets are blue,
the grass is greener,
except no football for you!

Xliner then logged off.
"Huh?" Nat said. "This doesn't make sense." She picked up a pen and wrote the rhyme down on a piece of paper. Maybe her friends could figure out what it meant. She clicked on "Compose Message."

From: NatSk8
To: WallIt, Kevlar, JamMan

Subject: Xliner

Check out this message from Xliner:

Roses are red,
violets are blue,
the grass is greener,
except no football for you!

I ran into him in the chatroom just a few minutes ago. Got any ideas what he's up to? All I can figure out is that he's still scuzzed out about football.

Later.

For Nat, it was harder waking up on Monday morning than on Saturday. She crawled out of bed like she was climbing from the grave. Across the room Ella was already dressed. She sat on her bed tying her shoes.

"Mom! She's awake!" Ella yelled.

Nat pulled her pillow over her head. "Do you have to shout?"

"Sorry," Ella said as she ran out of the room.

After taking a few minutes to recover from Ella's bone-jarring yell, Nat rolled out of bed onto the floor. She lay there on her back and tried to remember what day it was.

Mrs. Whittemore stuck her head in the room and looked at her daughter. "Hurry, Nat, or you'll be late for school."

Nat groaned. She sat up and waved her mom out of the room. "Blah, blah." Her long blond hair fell over her face.

47

By the time she was dressed, Ella had already left for school.

"How many times do I have to tell you? Hurry," Mrs. Whittemore insisted. She handed Nat her backpack and her fleece jacket. "There's no time for breakfast so eat this apple on the way." She shoved a red apple into Nat's hand.

Nat chomped on her apple all the way to school. She felt more like the living dead than a kid. "I hate Mondays," Nat said as she tossed the apple core into a garbage can.

When she arrived at school, the outside of the building was deserted. School had already started.

"Woof!"

Jamil's dog Buddy was sitting at the bottom of the steps to the main entrance.

"You better keep out of sight, fella," Nat said as she reached down and scratched his ears. "The principal hates pets."

"Woof!"

Nat headed into the school building and made her way to her first class. It was science. She wasn't worried about being late because she was really tight with Mr. Clary, the teacher. Outside of school she worked with him on the Bear Claw Mountain Bike Races.

As Nat slipped into the classroom and into her seat, Mr. Clary froze in front of the blackboard.

"I'm glad you could join us, Nat. Did you bring doughnuts?" Mr. Clary said.

The class laughed.

Nat looked surprised. "Doughnuts?"

"Yes. From now on if you're late for class, you'll have to bring us all doughnuts," Mr. Clary said. Then he turned his back on her and continued with his lecture on the sun. A big chart of the sun was pulled down in front of the blackboard. Mr. Clary held a pointer and was explaining the sun's different layers.

Nat glanced at the desk next to her. Kevin was sitting there taking furious notes. She half smiled because she knew he ate this stuff up. Nat, on the other hand, was only interested in getting a decent grade in the class. She could care less about science, but she wasn't going to let Kevin show her up by getting a better grade. Nat was very competitive in everything. She opened her notebook and started taking notes too. She'd have to copy the notes she missed from Kevin after class.

The fifty minutes of class went slow. Mr. Clary crammed so much information about the sun that Nat felt like her head was going to explode.

Rrrrring! The bell signaling the end of class sounded. Everyone slammed their notebooks shut and headed for the next one.

Nat grabbed Kevin's sleeve. "Got a sec?"

"I want to talk to you too," Kevin said. "I've been thinking about Xliner having no profile on the Net. I thought maybe Mr. Clary could give us some help on tracking this guy down."

"Good idea," Nat said. She totally forgot about asking her friend about copying his notes. "Mr. Clary! We need your help."

Mr. Clary sat at his desk as Nat and Kevin approached. "What can I do for you?"

"Well, we were wondering if you knew how someone could get on the Hoke Valley Net without leaving a trace," Kevin explained.

Mr. Clary raised his eyebrows. "Are you guys on another case?"

"Maybe," Kevin said. He didn't want to tell about the connection between Xliner and the lights going off at the stadium. "Right now, we just need to find out how it's possible that someone could get on the server without being officially signed on."

Mr. Clary steepled his fingers before his face. "I couldn't tell you, but why don't you call the HVNet? They should be able to help you. And if what you say is true, they'll want to know about it. The HVNet server is based at the university in Denver. Call there."

"Thanks, Mr. Clary," Kevin said as he and Nat headed into the hallway. They had three minutes to get to their next class.

"Maybe we can get the HVNet people to track Xliner," Nat said excitedly.

"I'll meet you after school and we'll call." Kevin disappeared down the hall. He had math on the other side of the building. If he ran, he would make it before the bell rang.

"Race you home!" Nat said to Jamil, Wall, and Kevin. School had just ended for the day. They were headed for Nat's house to call the people at HVNet.

Nat had a head start, but Kevin was coming up behind her. He was fast, real fast. Nat knew she could beat Wall and Jamil, but she would have to bust it to out-run Kevin.

As she headed down the block, she reminded herself not to look back over her shoulder. That was the killer in any race. It slowed you by at least a half a second, which could be the critical margin in beating someone. At the end of the block, she slowed to come around the corner at her street. She couldn't resist glancing out of the corner of her eye as she made the turn. Kevin was two feet behind her. And Buddy, Jamil's new dog, was coming up so fast he was going to pass them both.

But that wasn't what she should have been worrying

about. Just around the corner Roman Jacobson was coming.

Smack!

And that's who she ran into.

"Ugh." Nat bounced off Roman and into Kevin coming up right behind her. Kevin fell backward over Buddy. Buddy squealed.

"Sorry," Roman said.

Wall and Jamil slowed.

"You almost killed me, Roman," Nat said.

Roman shrugged. "Sorry, but I can't see around corners." He paused. "But I can do this." He held out a quarter in his right hand. "See this." He ran his left hand over it. The quarter disappeared.

"Cute," Nat cracked.

"Now, watch this," Roman said, ignoring Nat. He held his right hand out to Nat's ear, rubbed his fingers together, and a waterfall of coins spilled out of her ear.

"Cool!" Jamil said.

Roman smiled. He bent over and picked up his money. "Just a little entertainment for the masses."

"Thanks for the show, Roman, but we've got to jet," Nat said.

"If you're in a rush about the skate park, you might as well forget it. That park is not going to be built," Roman replied.

Nat's jaw dropped. "How would you know that?"

"My dad's the chair on the Zoning Board," Roman said.

"You're nuts," Wall cut in. "The Zoning Board has already voted for the park."

"The war isn't over until it's over." Roman smirked. "And let me tell you this is far from finished." Roman took off down the street.

Nat, Jamil, Wall, and Kevin stared at each other in shock.

"What's that supposed to mean?" Jamil asked.

"Beats me," Nat replied. "But I think he deserves watching more closely."

"You're jumping to conclusions again, Nat," Kevin warned. "He's a football player and his dad is against the park. Of course he's going to say something like that."

"Maybe you're right," Nat conceded. "Let's make that phone call."

The crew sat at the breakfast table while Nat made the call to Denver. The phone rang several times before someone at the HVNet picked up.

"Dr. David Dixon's office," a woman answered.

"Yes. I would like to speak to someone about the HVNet," Nat explained.

"Oh, you'll have to talk to Dr. Dixon about that," the woman said. "But he won't be back until next week."

"Is there some way I could reach him?" Nat asked.

"Well, he's at a conference for the next couple of days. Then he's spending the weekend up at his home in the mountains," the woman said as she ran through Dr. Dixon's schedule. "You could leave a message."

"Where is his mountain house?" Nat asked.

"In Hoke Valley, but he's not available up there," the woman explained. "He'll be back at work next week."

"That might be too late," Nat said. Then she left her name and phone number and told the woman it was urgent.

"So?" Wall said expectantly.

Nat sunk to the floor. "Dr. Dixon, the guy who runs HVNet, is out of town. He won't be back until next week." Nat twisted the phone cord. "At the rate things are going right now, that might be too late."

"Did the person tell you where his mountain house is?" Wall asked.

Nat nodded. "It's here, in Hoke Valley."

"Then let's check the phone book," Wall suggested.

"Why didn't I think of that," Nat said. She pulled the phone book out of the drawer and started rifling through it. "D's . . . d's . . . di's . . . dix's . . . ." Nat scanned the page. "It's not here. There's no Dr. David Dixon."

"Are there any other Dixons?" Kevin asked.

"Two others," Nat said.

"Let's call them," suggested Jamil.

Nat picked up the phone and dialed the first number. After a couple of rings, someone picked up.

"Is Dr. Dixon there?" Nat asked.

"You must have the wrong number," the person replied.

Nat dialed the second number.

It rang and rang and rang. No answer.

Nat shook her head. "What now?"

Her friends didn't answer.

"We're at a dead end with this," Kevin said.

"At least until next week," Nat reminded them. "Maybe he'll return my call."

"Well, that's our only lead to finding out who Xliner is," Wall said with disappointment.

"Unless we figure out what the riddle means," Kevin said.

"One thing it must mean is that Xliner's going to mess with football again. 'No football for you' is pretty clear I think," Wall concluded.

Nat looked at the clock on the stove. "I've got to run. The committee meeting is in half an hour."

Wall, Jamil, and Kevin headed to their homes to do their homework. Nat put on her in-line skates and headed to the high school. The committee was meeting in a classroom there.

Mayor Masters stood at the front of the room. Seven seats in the room were filled with the committee members, who included Ewan, Cyrus McGowan, Jane Kirby, an English teacher at the junior high and aunt to one of the raddest skateboarders in the country, Bob Williams, a retired ski slope operator, Brad Atkins, father of Nat's schoolmate Ian, Michelle Perkins, the director of the local Food Shelf, and Nat.

"First off, I have bad news," the mayor began.

Everyone groaned.

"Adam Jacobson filed a lawsuit this morning in county court to stop the skate park," said the mayor.

"How can he do that?" Nat said. "His own board

voted for the park!" She couldn't believe what she just heard. "That's got to be illegal."

"Calm down, Nat," the mayor advised. "Listen to what I have to say."

"I'm sorry," Nat apologized. Then she buried her chin in her chest and silently steamed.

"Adam represents a small faction right now. His suit argues that property values will drop and that a skate park is not the proper use for the land. He suggests that a hockey rink would be more appropriate."

"We should tear up the football field and put a hockey rink there," Nat interrupted.

Mayor Masters held up her hand to quiet Nat.

Nat glanced over at Ewan and she was surprised by what she saw. He didn't even seem to be paying attention. Instead, he was writing something in his notebook. That didn't make sense at all. If anyone here was committed to the skate park, it was Ewan.

Nat balled up a piece of paper and tossed it at him to get his attention. The paper landed on his desk, but Ewan simply brushed it away without looking up.

"Pssst," Nat whispered. "Ewan."

Again, Ewan ignored her so she focused back on the mayor.

"What we have to do is get the Zoning Board to commit to a timetable for the construction," the mayor explained. "Once we have that, there's not much Adam can do to stop us unless he gets an injunction from the court." She paused. "And I think that is highly unlikely."

The committee discussed a couple of other issues that had come up since their last meeting and then adjourned.

Afterward, Nat went immediately over to Ewan.

"Are you all right?" Nat asked with concern.

Ewan shrugged. "It's just like I said it would be. Coach Ham will win. He always wins. And nobody can stop him."

"It's not over yet," Nat said, trying to console Ewan.

"You got that right," Ewan said forcefully.

Nat looked at him funny. "What do you mean by that?"

"Nothing really. I just can't stand Coach Ham winning this," Ewan said. "I'd do just about anything to make sure he didn't."

Alarms went off in Nat's head. How far exactly would Ewan go? Is *he* the Xliner?

Ewan headed for the exit.

"Wait!" Nat called. She wanted to know more about what Ewan was up to but didn't know how to find out. Then she got a brainstorm. "Hey, why don't you come by my friend Wall's half pipe tomorrow. It totally rocks."

Ewan smiled. "That sounds super-good. I heard he had built one and I've been dying to try it out."

"It's perfect for aggro liners," Nat said.

"I'm tired of Ian's half pipe. It's just too wide for anything but bmx bikes," Ewan replied.

"Later, then," Nat said.

Ewan waved and disappeared down the hall.

After school the next day, the gang went straight to Wall's halfpipe. Ewan was meeting them there. Buddy met them at the school steps.

"Does that dog follow you everywhere?" Wall asked Jamil.

"Seems that way," Jamil answered. "At least the 'rents don't seem to mind. Turns out my dad likes dogs."

"Cool," Wall replied.

Buddy followed them to Wall's house.

"I can't wait to watch Ewan," Kevin said with excitement. "I bet he's really stylin' in the pipe."

"I'm too worried about the skate park to enjoy this afternoon," Nat sighed. "If only we could find Dr. Dixon. If Xliner does it again, he might turn everyone in town against the park. Then Coach Ham would win."

"Is there any chance Coach Ham is behind all this to turn people against the park?" Jamil asked.

Kevin shook his head. "Not Coach Ham. He's a total straight arrow."

"But his editorial sure did appear in the paper fast," Nat argued. "Too fast in my opinion."

"Maybe, but this just doesn't sound like Coach Ham," Kevin replied. "I really think he's a blind alley."

"What about someone thinking that they're helping him out," Wall suggested.

"Guys, yesterday I had a thought," Nat cut in. She was hesitant to bring this up, especially since she thought so much of Ewan. "Ewan is major pissed at Coach Ham and football. He thinks no matter what the committee does, the skate park won't be built."

"So? He's got a point," Kevin replied. "Coach Ham *is* a major obstacle."

"I know, but what struck me weird was when I was talking to him after the committee meeting last night. He said something about doing anything to stop the coach."

"And that could mean interrupting football games to get even for the park being stopped," Kevin finished Nat's thought.

"Right," Nat said. "So that's why I invited him today. I figured we could keep an eye on him. Maybe he'll let something slip."

"And I thought it was because you had a crush on him," Jamil cracked.

"Funny," Nat snapped.

"Don't be a jerk, Jamil," Kevin said.

"We could solve all of this if we found out who Xliner

was," Wall said trying to change the subject.

Jamil hopped onto a fire hydrant and stood with his finger in the air. "Wait, guys. I just might be able to solve that problem."

"How?" Nat asked sarcastically, still smarting from his last comment.

"You said Dr. Dixon lives up here in Hoke Valley and he's not in the phone book?" Jamil jumped off the hydrant.

Nat nodded.

"Well, besides having an unlisted number, there's another way a person can live up here and not have a number in the book. He could own one of the condos next to the slopes. Their phones come through the resort's switchboard," Jamil explained.

"Let's check it out!" Wall said.

"Wait! We're meeting Ewan first," Nat said. "Jamil can check tonight. Dr. Dixon isn't going to be in town until later this week."

At the halfpipe, Nat and Kevin put on their skates while Jamil and Wall warmed up on a couple of low ramps Wall had set up in the driveway. The X-crew had created a small street course in Wall's driveway. It consisted of a couple of boxes at different heights, a rail, and two small ramps.

Buddy took his position under the picnic table out of the sun.

Wall came off one of the ramps and pulled a 180 backside grab. He rotated weightlessly and landed fakie. Jamil followed with a frontside grab. He reached down and tweaked his board before sticking his landing.

By then, Kevin and Nat were ready.

Kevin skated fast and jumped up onto the rail, which was an old railroad rail they found in the woods and carried home. His skates splayed outward, grinding on the inside of his arches. An excellent alien soul.

Nat ignored the rail and jumped onto the two-foot-high box. Then, she came off it with a flying fish. One foot was tucked neatly under her while the other went straight out. She looked just like a fish leaping out of the water.

"Whoa!" She almost didn't stick the landing. Her skates wobbled as she tried to find her balance.

"She wiggles, she wobbles, but she don't fall down!" Jamil called.

Everyone laughed.

Suddenly, Buddy joined in with wild barking. "Woof! Woof! Woof!"

But when the crew stopped Buddy just seemed to intensify his barking. He stood and came out from under the picnic table.

"Woof! Woof! Woof!"

Just then, Ewan came into sight down the street. He was on his in-line skates. His arms swung methodically as he skated toward Wall's house.

When Buddy saw him, he took off down the street right at him.

"Buddy!" Jamil commanded. "Get back here, now!"

Buddy ignored Jamil's command.

Jamil ran after him, but the dog was well ahead.

Ewan spotted Buddy pretty quickly. He dropped into a crouch and went straight at the dog.

"I can't watch," Nat groaned as she covered her eyes.

Just as Ewan and Buddy were about to collide, Ewan leaped into the air and over the dog. While he was in the air he performed an awesome lu kang.

Buddy on the other hand stumbled face forward, snapping at empty space.

Ewan came straight onto Wall's driveway and jumped onto the rail. He ground a basic soul before hopping off. He skidded to a stop in front of Nat.

"Hey, Nat!" Ewan gave her a big smile.

"That was huge," Nat said.

By this time Buddy had turned around and was heading back, straight for Ewan again. As he barreled down the driveway, Jamil stepped in the way and wrapped his arms around the dog's neck.

"Calm down, boy," Jamil whispered in the dog's ear. "He's a friend."

"Woof!" Buddy strained to break free.

"I better get him out of here," Jamil said. "He doesn't seem to like Ewan."

"I have that effect on a lot of dogs," Ewan deadpanned.

Holding Buddy tightly by the collar, Jamil took off.

Nat, Wall, Kevin, and Ewan spent the rest of the afternoon skating. During the entire time, Ewan hardly said a word.

*   *   *

Across town a desk lamp clicked on. A pool of light spread across the desk. A hand pushed aside a stack of requisition forms waiting to be signed by Mr. Smith, the Hoke Valley Ski Resort manager.

Jamil reached over to the desktop computer and flipped the switch.

Jamil sat in his father's chair in his father's office in the belly of the resort. He was there to search the resort's files for an address on Dr. Dixon. His first guess that Dixon's phone went through the resort's main line was a bust. But now he hoped he could get an address for Dixon from the list of season pass holders. Dr. Dixon must have a season pass. Why else would he have a house up here in Hoke Valley?

Everybody in town was in his dad's database. He set up a search for "Dixon, David." The hard drive whirred as it searched. About thirty seconds later, Jamil hit pay-dirt. Dr. David Dixon, 144 Mountain Crest.

Jamil jotted down the address on a slip of paper. There was no phone number. That was strange, but he knew his dad's records weren't always complete.

As Jamil was about to switch off the computer, he noticed Dr. Dixon actually had three season passes. Jamil went to another screen to see who these belonged to.

Dr. Dixon's name came up, along with a woman's name . . . then came another name . . .

Ewan McKindrick!

Another lunch at Hoke Valley Junior High meant another disaster. The menu hung at the beginning of the line described what the school called food: macaroni and cheese, spaghetti and meatballs, fish sticks.

"Spaghetti, please," Nat told the server.

The server took a large spoonful of a bright orange concoction surrounding a ball of string. She dropped it on the plate and handed it to Nat.

"Thank you."

Wall was right behind Nat. He looked over her shoulder. "Just think. We have a whole year of this food to look forward to."

"That turns my stomach," Nat muttered. As she came to the register, Kevin waved to her from a table across the room.

Nat and Wall made their way through the crowded lunchroom to join them.

"Jamil has something important to tell us," Kevin said.

Just then Assistant Principal Mr. Hogg came up to the table. "Natalie Whittemore?"

Nat nodded.

"You're wanted in the office," said Mr. Hogg.

A deathly silence descended on the group. Being called to the principal's office was not a good thing.

"I didn't do anything," Nat pleaded.

"Hurry," Mr. Hogg said as he left to rain on someone else's day.

Her friends watched her leave the lunchroom like a condemned prisoner.

Nat hesitated in front of the door to the office. She hadn't been in there very often. Every time she had, it hadn't been a good experience. "Here goes nothing," Nat muttered under her breath. She swung open the door and entered the chaos of teachers and administrators hurrying around.

Mrs. Hickock looked up and noticed Nat. "Telephone." She pointed to the phone on her desk. "First button."

Nat froze. Why would she be getting a phone call at school? A list of possible catastrophes scrolled through her mind. She punched the blinking button.

"Hello?" Nat said nervously.

"Natalie? This is Mayor Masters. Something terrible has happened. Meet me and the rest of the committee at the football field after school," the mayor said hurriedly.

"What? What's wrong?" Nat asked with desperation.

But the only answer she got was a dial tone at the other end of the line. The mayor had hung up.

Nat's stomach knotted. She didn't think she could face lunch, so she disappeared into the library and pulled the letter *Q* of the encyclopedia from the shelf. Whenever she felt upset, she read the encyclopedia. She opened the book randomly and turned to a page that began with "Queeg, Captain."

After school Nat and her friends went straight across town to the high school. Buddy, as usual, tagged along. He had been waiting for Jamil outside of school all day.

As Nat and her friends entered the stadium, Buddy went nuts again and ran into the middle of the field. He was barking furiously. Jamil ran after him.

Nat, Wall, and Kevin climbed the stairs to the top of the stadium to where the other committee members were already seated. On the way up they passed Roman Jacobson sitting in the bleachers. He was playing cards with a couple of friends.

The whole committee was there, except for Ewan. Nat was surprised that he wasn't there. She couldn't believe he would miss it.

"What's wrong?" she asked out of breath. She squatted on a bench and breathed deeply. Wall, Jamil, and Kevin stayed a few feet behind her. This was Nat's committee not theirs, but they were just as concerned as Nat.

Coach Ham, who was with the others, pointed down to the field.

Nat followed his finger and gasped. In the middle of the field, at the fifty-yard line, the football that was painted on the grass was encased in a ring of brown, dead grass with a line of brown grass across it. It was the international sign for no. And right below that Sk8 was burned into the grass.

"No football," Nat said, reading the sign on the field. "Skate."

"Right, no football," Coach Ham repeated.

"We have a problem," the mayor interrupted.

"Get that dog off my football field!" shouted Coach Ham.

Buddy was barking up a storm and running in circles around the ring of dead grass. Jamil ran and caught Buddy by the collar and dragged him off the field.

The mayor waited until the coach settled down. "It has occurred to me that these incidents surrounding the football team are not isolated. These attacks on the football stadium, today and last Friday with the loss of power, seem to be happening right in the middle of the park controversy. According to the groundskeeper, the grass poison could have been applied anytime yesterday. No one was in the stadium and the football team did not practice." Mayor Masters glanced at Nat. "Now it seems logical that these pranks were committed by someone who likes skating. In light of this conclusion, I have no other option but to delay any further actions on the park until this is settled."

Nat gulped.

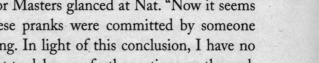

After the mayor's announcement the meeting quickly dissolved. Nat, Wall, and Kevin met Jamil in the parking lot.

"That was a brilliant move," Nat said to Jamil.

"It wasn't my fault," Jamil protested. "Buddy took off on his own."

Just then, Buddy took off again, but this time he stopped beside the door to the men's restroom. "Woof! Woof! Woof!"

"Well, the last thing we want to do is make Coach Ham any angrier, so you better keep that dog on a leash," Nat said.

When Jamil went over and grabbed Buddy, Ewan stepped out. He nodded to everyone.

Nat swallowed hard. She didn't know whether to be happy or angry. She still liked him, but what if he was behind this mess?

Buddy strained as Jamil held his collar tightly. He whimpered and tried to lunge at Ewan.

"Sorry, but I guess he doesn't like you," Jamil said to Ewan.

Ewan shrugged.

"Let's go someplace where we can talk," Wall said.

"Why not the field where the skate park is going to be?" Jamil suggested.

Nat gave Jamil a dirty look.

"What? What'd I say?" Jamil asked.

Nat sighed. "I'm sorry. It's not your fault. It's just that the skate park has been put on hold."

Jamil's eyes nearly popped out of his head. "You're kidding, right?"

"No," Ewan cut in. "But 'on hold' is just another meaning for never being built. It's just like I said. I knew the park would be canceled. Nobody would go against Coach Ham."

"Wait," Nat countered. "That's not why it's on hold. It's been delayed until they find out who did these things. You weren't at the meeting so you don't know."

Ewan just shook his head like she was too young to understand. He turned to leave.

His look crushed Nat. Now she had no chance of being his friend. Why would Ewan want to hang out with some little kid who didn't even understand how things were?

"Follow me," Kevin said as he pulled Nat along. He led her, Wall, and Jamil to the far edge of the field where the skate park was to be built.

Sticks with red flags marked the site. The crew sat in the middle of the space.

"This is where the halfpipe would have been," Nat said sadly.

"Don't give up yet," Jamil replied. "If we find the culprit, we can probably get the skate park back on track."

"That's right," Wall agreed.

Nat picked a blade of grass, put it between her thumbs, and blew. *Thwwwwpp!*

"I think Coach Ham hates skaters so much that he's doing this himself," Jamil said.

Kevin gave Jamil a weird look. "You're crazy, man. Coach Ham. He doesn't even jaywalk."

"Maybe, but how did he get that editorial in so fast," Nat said, picking up Jamil's argument. "And we've seen what he does to kids who skate on his team. He kicks them off. Look at what happened to Ewan."

"You're jumping to conclusions," Kevin reminded everyone. "We don't know if that's the real reason Ewan was kicked off the team. It's just what Ewan said."

"Well, let's ask Roman," Nat said. "He'd certainly know."

"Good idea," Wall said.

Jamil slapped his forehead. "I forgot to tell you guys at lunch. I got so distracted by Nat being called to the office. Ewan lives in the same house as Dr. Dixon. I found that out last night on my dad's computer."

"So he could have gotten on HVNet without leaving a footprint," Kevin said excitedly.

Nat groaned. The coolest in-line skater in town might also be a criminal. "It figures," Nat muttered to herself.

"What?" Wall asked.

"Nothing." Nat glanced at her friends. "Let's find Roman. He might still be around."

Roman was sitting on the hood of a big sedan in the school's parking lot. He was talking to the same two guys that he had been playing cards with earlier.

"Roman! Got a sec?" Nat called when she spotted him.

She, Jamil, Wall, and Kevin walked over.

"What's up?" Roman greeted them.

"Don't you have football practice?" Jamil asked.

"Canceled," Roman replied. "Coach was too bent about the field."

"We were wondering if you knew what got between Ewan and Coach Ham," Nat said.

Roman snorted. "Everything."

"Like what?" Nat pressed for details.

Roman shrugged. "Ewan wouldn't listen to Coach Ham. He wouldn't run the plays like the coach wanted him to. Instead, he'd run his own patterns and the quarterback could never find him."

"Football is a precision game," one of his friends said. "Unless everyone knows exactly what everyone else is doing, the whole play breaks down."

"Well, thanks," Nat said as she and the crew turned to leave.

"Wait!" called Roman. He held out a deck of cards. "Pick a card. Any card."

Nat smirked. "Okay." She picked a two of diamonds and showed it to her friends. Then she put it back in the deck.

Roman held the deck up to his forehead. "Two of diamonds."

"How'd you do that?" Nat gasped.

"A magician never reveals his secrets," Roman replied.

Nat and the crew left.

After they were a good distance from Roman, Jamil turned to his friends. "So it looks like Ewan might have lied about why he got kicked off the football team."

"Well, there are always two sides to every story," Nat countered. Even though she did believe that Ewan might be behind the pranks, she still felt a defensive urge toward him.

"So? What now?" Jamil asked. "I mean, it's got to be Ewan. He lives with the guy who runs the HVNet, and he has a major grudge against football."

"And don't forget he thinks that no matter what we do, the park won't be built," Nat added.

"Wait!" Jamil suddenly yelled. "That's not all. Remember how Buddy hates Ewan?"

Everyone nodded.

"Well, the only other time he's gone berserk like that was around the dead grass this afternoon." He looked at his friends. "So Ewan must have the same smell as the stuff that killed the grass. It's a total lock."

"If we could catch him with the grass killer," Nat replied.

"So, how *do* we catch him?" Wall asked.

"I don't think confronting him will do any good," Kevin said thoughtfully. "We'll have to catch him red-handed."

"I hate to bust such an awesome skater, but I guess we have to do it," Nat said. "But how?"

"He seems to have a flare for the dramatic. So the odds are that he won't do anything more until the game Friday night," Kevin concluded.

"We have to figure out what his next move is going to be," Wall said. "And there's only one way to do that."

"We can't follow him twenty-four hours a day," Jamil reminded everyone.

"I'm not suggesting we do. If you remember, Jamil, Ewan likes to boast in the chatroom and give clues to his next prank," Wall explained.

"So we take turns watching the chatroom," Nat said with a sense of triumph.

"In the meantime we've got to recover the support for the skate park," Kevin said. "Any ideas?"

They were all silent. No one seemed to have an answer.

Then Nat smiled. "Wall, you're going to like this." She patted her friend on his back "Let's have a skate exhibition at Wall's halfpipe. We can prove to everyone that skating is healthy and good for kids."

"Excellent!" Jamil agreed. "We could invite the entire Zoning Board and everyone else—including Coach Ham."

The next day the X-crew divided their time between school, organizing the exhibition, and monitoring the chatroom.

As usual Nat took charge of the exhibition. Jamil helped her out by making phone calls and putting up flyers around town.

Wall and Kevin focused on the Xtreme Sports Chatroom. They spent every waking moment in front of their computers waiting . . .

Until . . .

Wednesday afternoon, the day before the skate exhibition. Both Wall and Kevin were logged on when Xliner showed up in the chatroom.

Xliner: *Howdy, dudes!*
WallIt: *S'up, Sk8man?*
Xliner: *Life's a grind and I love it.*
Kevlar: *LOL.*
Xliner: *Just have a message to tell you.*
WallIt: *What now?*

Xliner: *Football players aren't just clueless, they're score-less!*

Xliner bounced out of the chatroom.

Kevlar: *He's gone.*
WallIt: *Yeah, but let's not take chances. Meet me at Nat's home.*
Kevlar: *I'm there.*

Nat was on the phone, while Jamil was scouring through a list of the key people they needed to contact.

"How's it going?" Wall asked as he and Kevin came into the kitchen.

"Great!" Jamil flashed a huge grin. "So far everyone is showing up, even Coach Ham and Mr. Jacobson."

"I thought those two would be impossible to convince," Kevin said.

"I know, but we're also trying to stack the audience with all the major skate fans around town," Jamil explained. "That way they can see how popular skating is."

Nat put her hand over the phone. "Cyrus has put up a big display in the window of Rumble Boards advertising it. The mayor even liked the idea."

"But I thought she had second thoughts," Wall said surprised.

Nat started speaking into the phone again.

"Now her second thoughts have had second

thoughts," Jamil replied.

"Then everything is set?" Kevin asked excitedly.

Jamil nodded.

"We've got good news, too," Kevin said.

"Well, sort of," Wall added.

"Yeah, Xliner is still out there. We got a hit in the chatroom about an hour ago," explained Kevin. "He said: 'Football players aren't just clueless, they're scoreless!'"

"What's that supposed to mean?" Jamil asked.

Wall shrugged. "I guess that's what we have to figure out."

"I've got to jet. I want to get some more work done on my science project," Kevin said.

"Just don't forget to bring your skates to Wall's house right after school," Jamil said.

"No way I'd miss it," replied Kevin. He descended down the stairs of Nat's apartment to the street.

Thursday afternoon the X-crew prepared for about fifty people to descend on Wall's yard.

"My dad is not thrilled," Wall said as the first spectators began to arrive. "He says it'll kill the grass." He had just set up his dad's stereo outside and plugged in a mike.

"It's for a good cause," Nat countered.

"That's what I told him. He said okay, but I have to reseed the lawn if it's ruined," Wall explained. "I told him you guys would love to help."

"Thanks for volunteering us," cracked Jamil.

Nat picked up the mike. "Welcome to the skate exhibition!"

People in the audience clapped. Coach Ham leaned over to Mr. Jacobson and whispered in his ear.

Nat noticed this and tried to ignore it. "First up is Jamil Smith. He'll perform some radical skateboard tricks for your pleasure."

Jamil climbed into the pipe, and the audience crowded around.

Perched at the edge of the lip, Jamil surveyed the pipe from above. He didn't want to mess up. "Here goes nothing." Jamil dropped into the pipe and rode up the opposite wall, turned, and went back up the other. Keeping his body low and his knees bent, he repeated this to pick up speed.

Suddenly, he popped high out of the pipe. Flying about six feet up in the air, Jamil spun a 360 with a toeside grab. He came back down into the pipe perfectly.

He felt a surge of confidence pulse through him. But he didn't have time to celebrate. He was shooting up the opposite wall at breakneck speed.

At the top Jamil twisted his deck sideways and fifty-fiftied about four feet of the lip before he dipped back down into the pipe.

"Pure, raw genius," Nat said into the mike.

Jamil went big. He sailed high out of the pipe and made a big grab.

"Alley-oop frontside air!" Nat said.

Jamil came down hard but stayed on his deck. He wobbled up the opposite side and came back down steadier.

Finally, Jamil dished out an awesome Cabbalerial, but the board slipped out from under his feet. He slid down the wall to the well of the pipe.

The adults in the crowd looked surprised as the kids went wild.

Jamil held his board over his head and jumped out of the pipe. The applause was deafening.

"Next up, Kevin Schultz," Nat announced. She was cranked by the crowd's response.

Kevin paused for a minute at the top of the pipe to gather his concentration. He wanted to one-up Jamil. And he knew that was going to be hard.

"One . . . two . . . go," Kevin said out loud. He dropped into the pipe and swung up the opposite side in a flash. His skates locked on the lip and flashed an effortless soul grind.

He was up the opposite wall where he crouched over his right skate and grabbed his left.

"Awesome fishbrain," Nat shouted excitedly.

Kevin came up out of the pipe lightning fast. In defiance of the laws of gravity, both his feet shot straight in the air. Kevin grabbed his skates forever! He twisted to land on his skates backward.

"The rocket!" Nat explained to the crowd.

Kevin came to the opposite lip and planted his hand on the cold metal. His skates popped high in the air for a sick invert.

But Kevin lost his balance and slid down into the pipe's well like a sack of potatoes.

"Ouch!" someone yelled from the audience.

Kevin raised his hand to indicate that he was okay.

Just then, Mayor Masters and Coach Ham pulled on Nat's sleeve.

Mayor Masters shouted over the noise, "Natalie, this

is incredible. I knew skating was fun, but I didn't know how hard it was. You guys must practice a lot."

"That's why we need a skate park—to practice."

Coach Ham nodded. "This takes a lot of skill. I thought it was just kids being reckless. I can appreciate this kind of effort."

"Thanks, Coach," Nat said, feeling incredibly relieved.

"After the new scoreboard is put up in the stadium tomorrow, let's sit down and talk about how I can help," Coach Ham said. He stuck out his hand. Nat shook it.

Kevin climbed out of the pipe. Now it was Wall's turn. Nat gave him a thumbs-up sign.

"So?" Kevin asked Nat.

"So Coach Ham is behind us!" Nat shouted to him.

"All right!"

"The coach wants to meet with us after the new scoreboard is put up tomorrow at the stadium," Nat explained.

"New scoreboard?" Kevin repeated.

Nat nodded.

"You know what that means, don't you?" Kevin continued.

"What?"

"Xliner's going to sabotage the scoreboard. Remember he said, 'Football players aren't just clueless, they're scoreless?'" Kevin asked.

"Oh, yeah!" Nat grinned. "We got him now!"

"This plan is aces, Kevin," Jamil said. He, Kevin, Wall, and Nat were entering the visitors' locker room at the football stadium. At the far end a crew of four men were installing the power box for the new scoreboard before that night's football game.

"See, Nat, science isn't a total waste," Kevin said as he turned to his friend.

"Okay, this time you're right, but I still think science is boring," Nat argued. "This light thing is pretty cool, I have to admit though."

Kevin held up the baby powder. "It will be impossible for Ewan to get this off unless he takes a shower and changes his clothes."

"And that will definitely be hard to do if he wants to hang around and watch the show," Wall added.

The construction workers were just finishing up with the box.

"Excuse me," Kevin said to one of the workers as he was about to close the control panel.

The guy turned with a questioning look.

"Coach Ham asked us to cover the inside of the panel with this baby powder," Kevin continued.

"What?" the guy asked with surprise.

Kevin explained that they expected someone to try to break into the panel this evening and the baby powder would help them catch the person.

The construction worker gave Kevin a look like he thought Kevin was crazy. "If the coach thinks it'll work, I'll let you do it," he replied skeptically.

Kevin nodded. "We're going to stake out the scoreboard, but as you can see this panel is difficult to watch because of its location." The panel for the scoreboard was hidden behind a wall in the men's locker room and the public bathroom, which was used by both spectators and the visiting team. "Hundreds of people will be passing by this panel."

"And we don't want to tip off the culprit before we catch him," Wall explained. "So we can't stand in front of it and wait."

"That makes sense," the guy admitted.

Kevin shook powder all over the door and the switches in the panel. Then he shook a circle of powder on the ground around the panel. "That should do it."

Nat nodded. "Let's get out of here." She looked around. "I don't want to be in here when the other team starts changing."

Wall, Jamil, and Kevin laughed.

"They won't be here for another hour," Wall said.

Nat looked at the clock on the wall. "We better get that light in place."

The crew then went outside the locker room. Jamil and Wall dragged a bench from inside the locker room and positioned it under the light over the door. Kevin stood up on the bench and dug a purple bulb out of his backpack.

"Are you sure this is going to work?" Nat asked.

"Absolutely," Kevin said forcefully. He screwed in the bulb. "This is a black light. The powder will stand out like it was glowing in the dark."

A purplish-blue light splashed across the doorway to the locker room.

"Now, Jamil and Nat, you position yourselves over there," Kevin ordered. "You'll have a perfect view from there."

"And you and Wall will watch the entrance on the other end of the locker room?" Jamil asked.

Kevin nodded. Then he and Wall carried the bench back into the locker room. Kevin replaced the light at the other entrance. Afterward they took up a position behind a Dumpster.

"Good choice, Kev," Wall complained. "I always like smelling rotting garbage."

Kevin smiled. "At least I didn't make you hide inside the Dumpster."

They laughed.

At the other entrance, Nat leaned against a wall. "This is boring."

"Yeah, but worth it," Jamil reminded her.

"I just wish we could go ahead and bust Ewan," Nat said.

"With what evidence? All the clues point to him, but we don't have anything concrete," Jamil replied. "We've got to catch him with his hand in the cookie jar."

"Rather, the powdered control panel," Nat cracked.

For an hour no one entered or exited the locker room. Then spectators started trickling into the stadium. A few men entered the locker room to use the bathroom. They came out with no sign of powder on them.

"Where's Ewan?" Jamil asked.

"I haven't seen him for a couple of days," Nat said. "I thought he'd be at yesterday's exhibition, but he was a no-show." She shrugged. She felt sad. She thought he was the coolest but now he was going to be taken down. She wished he had believed her when she told him the skate park wasn't a total bust.

They could hear the band warming up on the edge of the field. People in the crowd were clapping.

"I wonder how Kevin and Wall are doing," Jamil said.

"Why don't you check. I can cover this entrance," Nat suggested.

"Thanks. I'm definitely bored of waiting," Jamil said as he took off.

Nat leaned against a fence and didn't let her eyes stray from the door. She shifted her weight from foot to foot.

After a few minutes, the visitors' coaches came out of the locker room.

"No powder," Nat muttered.

A minute later, the entire visiting team came rushing out.

When she saw them, she almost had a heart attack. The entire team was wearing white and they all glowed like they were radioactive. If any of them had powder on their uniforms, Nat wouldn't be able to tell.

Her heart leaped into her throat. "Disaster," Nat groaned. She had to tell Kevin about this, but she didn't want to leave her post before Jamil returned.

Five minutes later Jamil appeared.

"Watch the door!" Nat called as she took off. She didn't have time to explain to Jamil about the visitors' uniforms.

At the other door Nat found Kevin and Wall lingering behind the Dumpster.

"You're going to ruin our hiding place," Wall complained when he saw her coming.

"Sorry, but this is important," Nat said. "The visitors are wearing white. They all glow in the black light."

"Ugh," Kevin groaned. "I guess I didn't think this through very well. Let's just keep an eye for Ewan and when he comes, we'll just have to follow him into the locker room and hope he doesn't notice us."

"Like I can do that?" Nat asked.

"Jamil can. You wait outside," Kevin said.

Nat nodded and returned to her post.

Finally, Ewan came into view. Nat grabbed Jamil. Ewan was heading straight for the locker room. He had his in-line skates slung over his shoulder and he didn't notice Nat or Jamil before he disappeared through the door.

Nat pushed Jamil. "Go!"

Jamil ran quietly to the door and then disappeared. Nat stood by the door and listened.

She got some strange looks from people passing, but she just ignored them.

Nat held her breath and tried to hear what was going on.

The sound of shoes scuffling echoed out of the locker room. Nat had to fight not to run in.

"We got him!" Kevin shouted from inside.

Then Kevin and Wall appeared with Roman between them.

"That's not Ewan," Nat shouted. "He's still in there!"

Kevin shook his head.

Nat pushed him aside and ran into the locker room.

The locker room was empty.

"Jamil!" Nat called frantically. "Where are you? Are you okay?"

"Over here!" Jamil answered from the other side of a row of lockers.

Nat ran over where she saw Jamil and Ewan sitting on a bench. Ewan was lacing up his skates.

"Grab him!" Nat ordered.

Jamil laughed. "You've got it wrong, Nat. It's not Ewan."

"It's Roman," Kevin said as he came up behind her.

Just then, Nat realized where she was and turned a deep shade of red.

Her friends laughed.

Nat left the locker room. Kevin followed her out. "Tell me everything, Kevin," she ordered.

"Roman was the one pulling the pranks. He's got the powder all over him."

With a look of deep embarrassment, Roman stood under the black light next to Wall. He looked like he had a bad case of radioactive dandruff.

"I don't get it," Nat replied. "I thought we had Ewan nailed for it."

"Me, too," Kevin said. He shrugged. "But we were wrong."

"Totally fooled is more like it," Roman taunted.

"But we still caught you," Wall replied. "Now spill it."

Roman smiled. "It was a beautiful thing. Everyone was supposed to think skaters were behind the pranks. Then the whole town would get behind Coach Ham and oppose the park. My dad says that if Coach Ham had the resources he could take us to the state championships again. This was supposed to help him get the resources."

Nat turned to Kevin. "Then what is Ewan doing in the locker room?"

"You won't believe this, but Ewan is going to give an exhibition at halftime," Kevin replied. "It was all Coach Ham's idea. He got Cyrus to pull out the half pipe he's got stored in his warehouse and they're going to set it up in the middle of the field. Ewan is going to rock the place out."

"Excellent!" Nat said. She turned back to Roman. "Now let's turn you over to Coach Ham. I'll bet he'll be surprised."

"Hoke Valley Miner fans, we have a special treat for you tonight," the announcer said over the loudspeaker as both teams returned to their locker rooms for halftime. A truck came out into the middle of the field dragging a small half pipe on a trailer. About twenty people lifted the pipe off the trailer and set it over the football-painted midfield. "Hoke Valley High's own Ewan McKindrick will perform an in-line skating exhibition for you. This is a taste of what's to come this spring when the new skate park is built next door."

The crowd applauded.

Ewan walked across the field and climbed into the pipe.

A rockin' tune was cranked up on the speakers.

Nat, Jamil, Wall, and Kevin stood along the sidelines. "This is incredible," Nat exclaimed.

Ewan took off like he was rocket-propelled. He came

high out of the pipe and pulled off a perfect flying fish. Then in a blink of the eye he was grinding a torque soul across the entire length of the lip.

Ewan then blasted out of the pipe for a monster McTwist.

"Never in my wildest dreams did I think I'd see Ewan skating at halftime on the fifty-yard line at a Miners' game," Nat said. She smiled as she watched him 720.

"This is definitely a strange world," Wall concluded.

"Especially when you hear the rest of the story," Jamil said. "Ewan told me that he was living with his grandparents while his parents worked for the Red Cross in the Philippines. He all but admitted to me that Coach Ham wasn't as bad as he let on. He didn't actually say it, but I got the feeling that he knew he was to blame for being thrown off the team. Apparently, he went a bit nuts in August when his parents took off and wouldn't listen to his grandparents or Coach Ham about anything."

"Oh, one of those I-know-what's-best-for-me things," Nat replied. She had done that lots of times.

Jamil nodded. "The weirdest thing was why Buddy went bonkers whenever he saw Ewan. Ewan has been putting sealant on his skates. They must smell as bad as the grass killer."

"So what about getting on the HVNet without a footprint?" Nat said. "And what about Coach Ham's editorial?"

"When I brought Roman to Coach Ham, he told the coach that he got on-line through the coaches' office,"

Wall explained. "It turns out there are lots of guest slots coded into the server. When a person uses one of those guest slots, they can put in whatever screen name they want and their footprint disappears when they sign off."

"And the editorial," Jamil continued, "was already written before the lights went out at the homecoming game. Coach Ham said all he had to do was call his friend, who also happened to be the editor in chief, and he was able to revise the story. As long as he kept his editorial the same length, he could change whatever he wanted to."

"Wow!" Nat exclaimed.

Just then, the crowd erupted in cheers. Ewan was pulling off a 450 mute transfer.

"Wow, again!" Nat repeated to herself, but this time she meant it about Ewan's awesome skating.

aggro: aggressive in-line skating

alien soul: a grind on the insides of both skates so that the skater kind of looks like an alien spaceship

alley-oop: when a trick is performed in the opposite direction from which the skater is going

Cabbalerial: while riding fakie, usually at the lip of a ramp, a completed 360 in the air landed heading back down the ramp face forward without grabbing. Named after Steve Cabbalero

deck: the platform of a skateboard

fakie: riding backwards

50-50: a double axle grind (a grind on both trucks) of a skateboard

fishbrain: same as flying fish but performed on the ground

flying fish: while catching big air, extending the right leg, tucking the left, and grabbing the right skate

grind: to scrape along the sides of an in-line skate on the lip of an obstacle

grind plate: a metal plate attached to the side of an in-line skate to protect the skate on grinds

invert: a trick where the head is beneath the skates

kung lao: while catching big air, extending the left leg, tucking the right one under, and grabbing the right skate by reaching over the left

lip: the top or upper edge of a ramp, half pipe, or obstacle

lu kang: while catching big air, reaching across the body and grabbing the opposite skate

McTwist: a 540-degree turn performed on a ramp. Named after Mike McGill

mute transfer: while catching big air, tucking both feet under and grabbing the opposite skate

rocket: while catching big air, grabbing the skate with both legs extended

suislide: a rockin' grind where the outside of the left skate scrapes the lip while the right leg is extended. Grab. Balance it, or crash!

torque soul: a cool grind on the outside of the left skate with the right skate perched on the inside of the left foot